HAVE FUN READING THIS BOOK!

IT OFFERS SOME REAL **SURVIVAL TIPS**. BUT THE SETTINGS **ARE NOT REAL**. **THINK** ABOUT HOW YOU CAN USE THESE **HACKS** IN REAL LIFE. USE **COMMON SENSE**. **BE SAFE** AND **ASK** AN **ADULT** FOR **PERMISSION** AND **HELP** WHEN NEEDED.

45th Parallel Press

Published in the United States of America by Cherry Lake Publishing
Ann Arbor, Michigan
www.cherrylakepublishing.com

Reading Adviser: Marla Conn, MS, Ed., Literacy specialist, Read-Ability, Inc.
Book Designer: Felicia Macheske

Photo Credits: © Jacky Co /Shutterstock.com, cover; © Liubou Yasiukovich/Shutterstock,com, cover; © Kamira/Shutterstock.com, 5; © Guadalupe Rodriguez/Shutterstock.com, 6; © Phira_60/Shutterstock.com, 9; © Triff/Shutterstock.com, 11, 14, 15; © Ultrashock/Shutterstock.com, 13; © SlayStorm/Shutterstock.com, 14; © SeeSaw GmbH/Shutterstock.com, 17; © exopixel/Shutterstock.com, 21; © Aprilphoto/Shutterstock.com, 21; © Alyona Sunny/Shutterstock.com, 22; © Levent Konuk/Shutterstock.com, 23; © Krasowit/Shutterstock.com, 25; © Alla V/Shutterstock.com, 29

Other images Throughout: © © SrsPvl Witch/Shutterstock.com; © Igor Vitkovskiy/Shutterstock.com; © FabrikaSimf/Shutterstock.com; © bulbspark/Shutterstock.com; © donatas1205/Shutterstock.com; © NinaM/Shutterstock.com; © Picsfive/Shutterstock.com; © prapann/Shutterstock.com; © S_Kuzmin/Shutterstock.com © autsawin uttisin/Shutterstock.com; © xpixel/Shutterstock.com; © OoddySmile/Shutterstock.com; © ilikestudio/Shutterstock.com; © Kues/Shutterstock.com; © VectorsMarket/Shutterstock.com; © ankomando/Shutterstock.com; © Macrovector/Shutterstock.com; © ArnaPhoto/Shutterstock.com; © Olga Axyutina/Shutterstock.com

45th Parallel Press is an imprint of Cherry Lake Publishing.

Library of Congress Cataloging-in-Publication Data

Names: Loh-Hagan, Virginia, author.
Title: Deserted island hacks / by Virginia Loh-Hagan.
Description: Ann Arbor, MI : Cherry Lake Publishing, [2019] | Series: Could you survive? | Includes bibliographical references and index.
Identifiers: LCCN 2019006164| ISBN 9781534147805 (hardcover) | ISBN 9781534150669 (pbk.) | ISBN 9781534149236 (pdf) | ISBN 9781534152090 (hosted ebook)
Subjects: LCSH: Wilderness survival–Juvenile literature. | Survival–Juvenile literature. | Islands–Juvenile literature.
Classification: LCC GV200.5 .L64 2019 | DDC 613.6/9–dc23
LC record available at https://lccn.loc.gov/2019006164

Cherry Lake Publishing would like to acknowledge the work of The Partnership for 21st Century Skills. Please visit *www.p21.org* for more information.

Printed in the United States of America
Corporate Graphics

Dr. Virginia Loh-Hagan is an author, university professor, former classroom teacher, and curriculum designer. She's been to several islands. She's been to the Hawaiian Islands. She's been to Caye Caulker. She's been to Whidbey Island. But she stayed in hotels. She lives in San Diego with her very tall husband and very naughty dogs. To learn more about her, visit www.virginialoh.com.

INTRODUCTION 4

CHAPTER 1
BLOCK THE SUN AND BUGS! 11

CHAPTER 2
FIRE A SIGNAL! 15

CHAPTER 3
MAKE DRINKING WATER! 19

CHAPTER 4
CATCH FISH! 23

CHAPTER 5
MAKE SHELTER! 27

DID YOU KNOW? 30
CONSIDER THIS! 31
LEARN MORE 31
GLOSSARY 32
INDEX 32

COULD YOU SURVIVE ON A DESERTED ISLAND?

THIS BOOK COULD SAVE YOUR LIFE!

Deserted means empty of people. **Islands** are lands surrounded by water. Water is on all sides.

Deserted islands are in the middle of oceans. They're far away from cities. They're far away from people. It'd be hard to get to the closest land. It'd be too far to swim. It'd be too far to get to without a boat.

Deserted islands have many dangers. They have wild animals. They have poisonous plants. The weather can be extreme. They can be really cold. They can be really hot.

TIP Learn all you can about different places.

There are 2 main ways you could end up on a deserted island. One way is from a plane crash. Planes fly over oceans. If they crash, they'll land in the water or on an island. There are many islands in the sea. Some islands aren't even on maps.

A shipwreck could also lead you to a deserted island. Ships travel in the sea. If something happens to the ship, you could get lost at sea.

Either way, you're alone. You're **stranded**. Stranded means left to survive on your own.

TIP Search the area. Collect any useful things.

You might be one of the lucky survivors. You have to be smart. First, know how to use the island. Second, know how to use the sea. Third, don't get too lonely. Don't lose your mind. Keep busy. Have a plan.

Most importantly, know how to survive. Keep this in mind:

- You can only live 3 minutes without air.
- You can only live 3 days without water.
- You can only live 3 weeks without food.

This book offers you survival **hacks**, or tricks. Always be prepared. Good luck to you.

TIP Keep your cell phone. Check for signals. You never know.

SCIENCE CONNECTION

It's odd to be surrounded by water and not be able to drink it. Seawater has too much salt. Humans can only have small amounts of salt. They usually have salt with water and other foods. This spreads out salt. It keeps it at a healthy level. The salt in seawater is higher than what humans can process. Living cells inside humans need a little salt. But too much salt can be deadly. Human kidneys make pee. They get rid of extra salt. To drink seawater, humans would have to pee more than they drink. This makes humans thirstier than before. They'd become dehydrated. Dehydrated means their bodies don't have water. Kidneys would stop working. Drinking seawater causes many problems. It increases blood pressure. It increases heart rate. It makes breathing hard. It increases sweating. It causes pains. It damages the brain. It makes people pass out. It can lead to death.

CHAPTER 1

BLOCK THE SUN AND BUGS!

Oh no! The sun is burning your skin. It can damage your body. Its heat can make you sick. And bugs are biting you. You need relief! Make your own sunscreen and bug spray.

HACK

1. Get a pile of dirt. Add water. Mix. Make mud.
2. Collect plants that keep away bugs. Examples are mint and lavender. Plants that smell like lemon would also work.
3. Rub the plant leaves. This releases the oils. Grind into a paste.
4. Add the plant paste to the mud. Mix together.
5. Spread the mud mixture all over your body. Cover your skin. When it dries out, spread more.
6. To make extra strong, add coconut oil. Add fish or animal fat. Wrap wet seaweed on top.

TIP Find aloe vera. This plant heals burnt skin.

explained by

STEM

The key to this hack is the mud.

Mud is **opaque**. Opaque means that it can't be seen through. Mud acts like a physical barrier. It protects your skin. It blocks the sun's rays. It doesn't let light through.

It also blocks your smell from bugs. Our bodies make smells. Bugs can smell sweat, **odors**, and gases. Odors are smells. Bugs use these smells to find victims. They can smell as far as 100 feet (30 meters) away. Mud and plants block your smells. They clog up bugs' **receptors**. Receptors are the senses used to smell.

CHAPTER 2

FIRE A SIGNAL!

Use rocks to write **SOS** on the beach. SOS means help. Also, build a fire. Smoke is a help signal. You'll need fire to stay warm and cook food too.

TIP Use smoke to keep bugs away.

HACK

1. Gather sticks and **tinder**. Tinder is needed to start fires. Examples are twigs, leaves, or coconut fibers.
2. Create a teepee shape with the sticks.
3. Find wood. Use a sharp rock. Cut a groove on a piece of wood.
4. Put tinder on the groove.
5. Use a hard stick. Rub up and down along the groove.
6. Rub until the tinder smokes. Blow on the smoke to catch fire.
7. Put smoky wood under teepee. Put tinder on top. Add more sticks and tinder.
8. To make smoke, burn damp wood.

explained by STEM

The key to this hack is friction.

Friction is the rubbing of one thing against another thing. It's the resistance to motion. While one thing is moving, the other thing is resisting. No surface is smooth. When 2 surfaces rub against each other, they get caught on each other. Friction causes the energy of the motion to turn into heat. Rubbing 2 sticks together makes fire.

To make fire, we need fuel, oxygen, and heat. The fuel is the sticks. The oxygen is the air. Friction is the heat. When enough of these things are present, fire happens.

TIP Use a mirror to get attention. A mirror can shine a light beam up to 10 miles (16 kilometers).

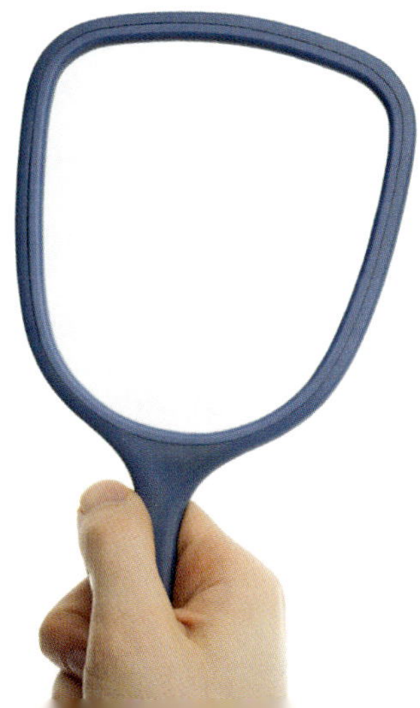

REAL-LIFE CONNECTION

Okunoshima Island is off the coast of Japan. It's isolated. It's far enough from people. It's secure. At first, only 3 fishing families lived on the island. In 1894 to 1895, Russia and Japan fought against each other. Ten forts were built on the island. During World War II, a chemical weapons factory was built on the island. It made poison gas for the Japanese army. It tested the gas on rabbits. This was a secret mission. Japan lost the war. The gas was dumped. Records were destroyed. The rabbits were released. The island was deserted. Today, wild rabbits are all over the island. It's called Rabbit Island. No humans live there. In 1988, Japanese went back to the island. They created a poison gas museum. Visitors take a boat to the island. There are campsites. There are walking trails. People can feed the rabbits. But they can't hunt them. Dogs and cats are not allowed.

CHAPTER 3

MAKE DRINKING WATER!

Water is all around you. But you can't drink it. Seawater will make you sick. You need freshwater. Islands have a lot of plants. That's a good sign. There may be water in vines. There's also water in fruit. Collect water from plants.

HACK

1. Get palm leaves. Tear into strips. Braid together. Make a rope.
2. Get a clear plastic bag. (Search the island for trash.)
3. Tie the bag on the end of a plant or small tree branch. Make sure the bag is sealed tightly. Make sure the bag doesn't leak.
4. Leave out all day long. Leave it out for the sun.
5. Take the water out at night. You'll get 1 cup (250 ml) of water per bag.

TIP Go inland. Find freshwater. Look for small streams. Look for waterfalls. Look for water in caves. Boil water before drinking.

explained by

STEM

The key to this hack is the water cycle.

Water changes forms. It becomes a **liquid** or water form. It becomes a **vapor** or gas. It becomes ice or **solid**. The sun heats up the Earth. This makes the ocean temperature rise. Some of the ocean water **evaporates** into the air. Evaporate means water changes to gas. Plants sweat through their leaves. This process is called **transpiration**. As water vapor rises, it cools. It becomes a liquid. This process is called **condensation**. The bag is full of **saturated** vapor. Saturated means full of water. This changes vapor into water. This process is called **precipitation**. The fallen precipitation is at the bottom of the bag.

TIP Collect water from rain and storms.

CHAPTER 4

CATCH FISH!

The sea has plenty of food. Look for small sea critters around **shallow** water. Shallow means not deep. For bigger fish, make a fishing line.

TIP Always cook your food. Make sure it's not poisonous.

HACK

1. Get something that you can use as a hook. Use a sharp twig. Other examples are paper clips, broken soda tops, or hairpins.
2. Twist the item into a hook shape.
3. Get something that you can use as a fishing line. Use long plant stems. Use thread from your clothes. Other examples are shoelaces or string.
4. Tie the line to the hook.
5. Add bait to the hook. Use food scraps. Use shiny things.
6. Dangle the hook in the water. Hold on to the line. Wait for fish to bite.

TIP Rub food on your skin before eating. Wait a bit. Check to see if you have a reaction.

explained by

STEM

The key to this hack is tension.

Tension means being stretched tight. It's a **force**. It's used to stretch things out. Forces are a push or pull. They're applied on things. Forces change the positions of things. They change the speed of things.

When a fish is on the line, tension is present. The fish puts weight on the hook. This pulls the line tight. Tension is created. If there's too much tension, the line could break. This is why you should scoop fish with your hands or a container. Don't pull on the line or it'll break.

SPOTLIGHT BIOGRAPHY

Amelia Earhart was born in 1897. She was a famous aviator. Aviators fly planes. Earhart flew across the Atlantic Ocean. She did this by herself. She was the first woman to do this. In 1937, she tried to fly around the world. She disappeared over the Pacific Ocean. Nobody knows what happened to her. Some people believe she died in a plane crash. Some believe she survived an emergency landing. Earhart may have lived on a deserted island. She may have died on the island called Nikumaroro. Human bones were found there. Scientists studied the bones. They think it's a match for Earhart. This island is about 4.5 miles (7 km) long. It's 1.5 miles (2.4 km) wide. It's about 1,000 miles (1,609 km) from Fiji. It's halfway between Australia and Hawaii. Earhart's death is still a mystery.

CHAPTER 5

MAKE SHELTER!

Get out of the sun. Protect yourself from the weather. Protect yourself from animals. Stay safe until you're rescued. Make shelter. Stay close to a water source. Stay close to the shore. You don't want to miss any planes or ships.

HACK

1. Find a large branch.
2. Lean one end against a tree. This will be your roof line.
3. Get smaller branches. Lean the branches against the main branch. Make a triangle shape. Crisscross the tops of the branches. This is like your walls.
4. Make rope from plant strips. Tie the tops of the branches together.
5. Cover the top with branches and leaves. This will protect you.
6. Put soft leaves on the inside floor. This will be your bed.

TIP Build away from coconut trees. You don't want a coconut falling on your head!

explained by

STEM

The key to this hack is its design.

The design depends on **angles**. Angles are the spaces between 2 crossing lines. They're the points where 2 lines meet.

You need to think about your height. Your shelter should fit your size. It shouldn't be any bigger. The bigger the space, the harder it is to keep warm. This is because of heat loss.

The main branch should be at an angle that fits your height. It should be a little above your head when sitting. The wall branches should go down the length of the main branch. They should be at a 45-degree angle.

TIP Rest. Plan your next moves. Stay alive.

DID YOU KNOW?

- John F. Kennedy is the only U.S. president who was stranded on an island. In 1943, Kennedy fought in World War II. He was a Navy officer. His boat was hit by the Japanese. Kennedy and his surviving crew swam 3.5 miles (5.6 km). They swam for 4 to 5 hours. They swam to Plum Pudding Island. This island was deserted. It's in the Pacific Ocean. Kennedy and his men lived on the island for a couple of days. They ran out of food and water. They swam to a bigger island. They lived there for a couple more days. They ate a lot of coconuts. They were rescued. Today, Plum Pudding Island is referred to as Kennedy Island.

- In 2014, a fake news story circulated about Gemma Sheridan. It said she had spent 7 years on a deserted island. She made an SOS sign. A kid in Minnesota was on Google Earth. The kid saw her sign. That's how she was saved. It turns out this was made up. The news source was not real. The pictures were from another news story.

- Daniel Defoe was an English writer. He wrote *Robinson Crusoe*. He did this in 1719. This book is the most famous story about a deserted island survivor. It has inspired many movies, TV shows, and books. These stories are called Robinsonade.

- People can pay money to be deserted on an island. There are companies that sell survival experiences. They take people to a deserted island. They create situations for them. They leave them to take care of themselves. But they watch people. They make sure people don't get hurt.

- Many islands have coconuts. Coconuts are very useful. They're a source of water and food. The shells can be used for bowls and armor. Coir is the fiber from the coconut shell. It can be used to make ropes, beds, blankets, and clothes. Coconut leaves can be used to make brooms and baskets. Coconut oil is good for the skin.

CONSIDER THIS!

TAKE A POSITION!

Botany is the science of plants. Physics is the study of how things work. Medicine is the study of healing. Which science is the most important for survival on a deserted island? Argue your point with reasons and evidence.

SAY WHAT?

In an emergency, it's important to not panic. The Boy Scouts use a code. It's called "STOP." S means "stay calm." T means "think." O means "observe." P means "plan." Explain how you would use STOP if you were trapped on a deserted island.

THINK ABOUT IT!

"What would you bring to a deserted island?" This is a popular question. Think about your answer. If you could only bring 3 things, what would they be? Why?

LEARN MORE!

Bell, Samantha. *How to Survive on a Deserted Island*. Mankato, MN: Child's World, 2015.

O'Shei, Tim. *How to Survive on a Deserted Island*. Mankato, MN: Capstone Press, 2009.

Pipe, Jim. T*ough Guides: How to Survive on a Desert Island*. New York, NY: PowerKids Press, 2013.

GLOSSARY

angles (ANG-guhlz) spaces between two crossing lines, points where two lines meet

condensation (kahn-den-SAY-shuhn) the process of water collecting as droplets on a cold surface when humid air is in contact with it

deserted (dih-ZUR-tid) empty of people, uninhabited

evaporates (ih-VAP-uh-rates) changes from water into gas

force (FORS) push or pull

friction (FRIK-shuhn) the resistance that one surface or object encounters when moving against another surface or object

hacks (HAKS) tricks

islands (EYE-luhndz) bodies of land surrounded by water

liquid (LIK-wid) water form

odors (OH-durz) smells or scents

opaque (oh-PAKE) not able to be seen through, not transparent

precipitation (prih-sip-ih-TAY-shuhn) the process where vapor becomes water

receptors (rih-SEP-turz) organs that receive senses

saturated (SACH-uh-rate-id) full of water

shallow (SHAL-oh) not deep

solid (SAH-lid) a form that is firm and stable in shape

SOS (ES-OH-ES) universal sign for help, distress signal

stranded (STRAND-id) left to survive on one's own

tension (TEN-shuhn) the state of being stretched

tinder (TIN-dur) things used to start a fire, like wood or paper

transpiration (tran-spuh-RAY-shuhn) the process where plants absorb water through the roots and then give off water vapor through pores in their leaves

vapor (VAY-pur) gas form

INDEX

angles, 29

bug spray, 11–13

coconuts, 28, 30
condensation, 21

deserted islands, 4–9, 26, 30
drinking water, 19–21

Earhart, Amelia, 26
evaporation, 21

fire, 15–17
fishing, 23–25
force, 25
freshwater, 19–21
friction, 17

Kennedy, John F., 30

mud, 12, 13

opaqueness, 13

precipitation, 21

Rabbit Island, 18
receptors, 13
Robinson Crusoe, 30

salt, 10

shelter, 27–29
sunscreen, 11–13
survival, 8

tension, 25
transpiration, 21

vapor, 21

water, 19–21